THE WATSONS BEGINNINGS

COURTSHIP & MARRIAGE

The Watsons Beginnings

Arc Two:

Fortune & Family

A Prequel to *Refined and Returned*

Eireanne Michaels

Cover Art: "My Lady is a Widow and Childless" by Marcus Stone
Edited by Marijke Kriel
ISBN-13: 978-1-969841-06-4
First Edition: May 2026
LITERARY REALMS PRESS

Disclaimer: This is a work of fiction. Unless otherwise indicated, all names, characters, businesses, places, events, and incidents in this book are either the product of the author's imagination or used in a fictitious manner. The author does not speak for or represent the people, companies, corporations, or brands mentioned in this book. While this work may incorporate historical figures and events, it is a dramatized interpretation and not intended as a factual account. Any characterizations, dialogue, or events are fictionalized for storytelling purposes.

Table of Contents

Preface

This story is a prequel to *Refined and Returned* by Eireanne Michaels, a completed version of *The Watsons*—the unfinished fragment by Jane Austen. Written on paper with watermarks from 1803 and 1804, *The Watsons* was set aside by Austen for reasons unknown and never completed. While many have speculated on why she abandoned it, the truth remains a mystery.

The original manuscript is preserved in:

MS. MA 1034, Morgan Library & Museum, New York

MS. Eng. e. 3764, Bodleian Library, Oxford

Eireanne Michaels has completed *The Watsons* by adhering to Austen's style, allowing her characters to act within the personalities Austen crafted. In developing the novel, the author created a detailed backstory for the Watson family, spanning three decades before the events of *Refined and Returned.* This prequel is part of that story.

Arc Two:

Fortune & Family

This story is dedicated to—all the people who have had to make sacrifices to protect those they love, especially when the other party was unaware of what you did for them.

Prologue

Omniscient

The Reverend Mr Watson and his wife had lived happily on a small income for several years, though the family seemed to grow more quickly than the means to support it. Mr Watson often counted himself blessed in frugality, and Mrs Watson, having endured the consequences of her first husband's vices, was willing to follow his lead. Mrs Watson was a devoted wife and mother who made sure all their children were seen, heard, and loved—while Mr Watson struggled with understanding and coping with their differing personalities. In addition, each new child brought fresh expenses—their clothes, shoes, and overall semblance of gentility relied on the generosity of the Turners of *Kyrkelidun* and the extended Willoughby family which galled Mr Watson's pride and his wife's independent spirit.

The patronage of Mr Watson's uncle—Sir Charles Turner, 1st Baronet of *Kyrkelidun*—and his brother-in-law, Henry Willoughby—then Baron Middleton, later extended to the

Watsons' sons and daughters in other ways. In 1782, when Robert Jr turned eleven, he matriculated at Beverley Grammar School—his godfather's Alma mater. A year later, in September 1783, Elizabeth was sent to a girls' seminary in York, where she remained for the next three years. Though school fees were covered by relatives, easing the family's expenses, each departure deepened the heartache of separation—especially after Sir Charles's death, a month after Elizabeth left for school.

In his will, Sir Charles named Mr Watson as the principal guardian of his children and estate, further adding to the Watsons' domestic duties. It was only with the occasional assistance of the *Briddhalh* Willoughbys providing transportation that Mr and Mrs Watson could visit their eldest son and daughter during their school holidays. Then, in November 1784, the widowed Mrs Turner remarried Sir Thomas Gascoigne, Baronet, and took her three children to live at his estate of *Perlintun.* This left Mr Watson with only the Turner estate to oversee—a burden in its own right, though it demanded less of his time than child-rearing. Yet the separations grew longer: Robert Jr and Elizabeth spent most holidays at school or with friends, and Mrs Watson's bouts of melancholy worsened with their absence.

Mrs Watson's distaste for being separated from her children only deepened when, in January of 1786, she was summoned to *Perlintun* at the behest of Lady Gascoigne. Her old friend was suffering from complications following the birth of her son, Thomas, and longed for the comfort of familiar company. Yet nothing Mrs Watson could do availed; Lady Gascoigne passed in early February, leaving Sir Thomas devastated. A widower with an heir, he had no intention of remarrying and thus offered to continue raising the Turner children, to whom he had grown attached. However, as there was no mistress or other female relative to oversee the education of the girls, it was decided that they would return to *Kyrkelidun* and, like young Charles, would spend half their holidays at *Perlintun.*

Mrs Watson returned home weak and wan; her spirit further diminished by the loss of her friend. That summer, when Elizabeth finally completed her schooling and returned home, the Watsons decided to send Penelope to a smaller, less prestigious seminary in Stockton-On-Tees from September, where her family could more easily visit.

But Mrs Watson's resilience—already tested—shattered entirely, the following summer, when Mr and Mrs Edward Turner of Shropshire visited the Watson family with a proposal.

Chapter One

Unexpected Guests

Mrs Watson

— Pall Mall, London

Sunday, July 1787

My Dear Brother,

I take up my pen to apprise you that we are presently occupied with preparations to vacate this wearisome metropolis, for the Season has concluded—or, at the very least, all persons of quality have already taken flight. We shall quit London on the 'morrow and are bound for Shropshire—though we are resolved to divert our journey so as to bestow a visit upon our family in Yorkshire. Though the remoteness of the country is inconvenient to us, I trust you shall derive sufficient pleasure from our visit to render it worthwhile. Thus, you may anticipate our arrival towards the close of the week.

I shall dispatch this missive with the morning post before we depart, so that you may have ample time to prepare for our arrival. I must insist that you endeavour to have the house in some semblance of order—though I know not how you will manage with so many children about the place—as I still remember the disarray in which we found you on our last visit.

Give my love to my dearest sister-in-law, and look for us at the end of the week.

Yours affectionately,
M. Turner

The letter from Mrs Turner was delivered on Thursday, leaving the Watsons little time to prepare. With no idea when their unexpected guests would arrive, the whole family pitched in to clean, prepare the guest room, and send to town to fill the larder before the carriage pulled up at their door on Saturday afternoon.

After greeting their relations and seeing to the stowing of their luggage and the placement of their carriage, they all returned indoors where they soon sat down to dinner.

While they dined, Mrs Turner spoke for some time about their recent forays during the London season in her usual monologue, only occasionally allowing her husband to speak a word or two of explanation over one matter or another before she waved him off and continued. Once she finished eating, she turned to the children who had been unusually quiet—her voice cutting through their silence like a knife. "Pray, leave your elders to converse, and do endeavour to conduct yourselves with a modicum of decorum, lest you become a source of unwelcome commotion." With a look at their parents for approval, the children removed to the parlour.

Once they were out of the room, Mrs Turner continued on in her callous manner, "My dear brother and sister, you simply must accept our offer. I confess I cannot conceive how you have managed so long with so numerous a family upon such a trifling income. It is surely a matter that deserves our most earnest consideration and aid."

Mrs Watson tried not to cringe at her sister-in-law's manner of insinuating that she wished to help them while insulting their way of life, not to mention her lack of consideration in trying to arrange their lives. She knew it was simply Mrs Turner's way, but she still had trouble not retaliating against her. She had never liked her husband's youngest sister; however, she managed to school her expression and asked, "Exactly what is this offer that you speak of, Margaret?"

Mrs Watson was always careful to keep her distaste for Mrs Turner from showing on her face and in her voice; however, she absolutely refused to sully the word 'sister' or any other endearment by using them to speak of this woman. Though, luckily, Mrs Turner had never noticed or commented on it.

"What offer? My dearest sister, I find myself quite dismayed; pray tell, have you not listened to a single word I have said?" She said with exaggerated exasperation. "Perhaps, my words have been but idle whispers upon the wind, failing to completely capture your attention?"

Mr Watson's expression showed his pique at his sister's way of speaking to his wife, and Mrs Watson took heart from knowing that he would throw his sister out on her behalf if she wished; however, she did not want to be the reason for a break in the family—especially if the Turners actually had an offer that proved beneficial. While Mrs Turner could not be relied upon for any such thing, Mr Turner was an immensely sensible man in everything except his choice of wife. However, Mrs Watson knew how Mrs Turner had fooled the man in order to marry his fortune, and she felt too sorry for him to allow her husband to turn them out. So, she clasped her husband's arm between her hands and gave it a gentle, insistent squeeze, hoping to draw away his attention and soothe his agitation.

Mr Turner then took up the conversation as he tried to mollify his hosts with a proper explanation. "As you know, your sister and I have been married for some years, and there has been no sign of a child being forthcoming. Therefore, we—"

"We have decided to take on a ward. Our objective is to raise and educate the child as our intended heir," interrupted his wife, who had given up on her false distress to retake the main role in the conversation. "And what could be more sensible than for us to offer succour to one of your own? For Mr Turner's relations are, I must confess, few in number and, by all accounts, comfortably established; whilst my own dear brother finds himself burdened with an abundance of offspring and, I fear, without a legacy to bequeath to any of them."

Mr and Mrs Watson were stunned by the suggestion that Mrs Turner was making. They turned to Mr Turner—who blushed at his wife's lack of decorum in making it. However, Mrs Watson could feel her husband tense at his sister's final words. That Mrs Turner should insult her brother—and in his own home—the audacity of it was astounding! But Mrs Watson swallowed her own indignation in order to pacify her husband's. She drew a steadying breath and began to stroke his arm with deliberate gentleness, willing the tension from his muscles in another attempt to alleviate his rising temper. They both sat in such a manner for some minutes—though Mrs Turner continued on in her nonsensical way; however, the couple could not respond due to the deafening roar in their ears which nearly drowned out her voice.

Mr Turner realised their anger first, to no one's surprise, and he interrupted his wife, "My dear, were not you telling me how fatigued you were from all our recent travel? Why do not you go lie down, and I will send Millie to tend you. I believe we should give our brother and sister some time to consider our offer which will give you plenty of time to relax."

His soothing voice finally broke through Mrs Watson's haze, and—as much as she pitied him—she appreciated Mrs Turner's choice of husband. Mrs Turner at first refused to admit she had ever said anything of the like, but Mrs Watson would not let such an opening go without a fight.

"Oh, Margaret, I do apologise," she said in a falsely sweet voice. "I had not even considered how tired you must be having travelled all the way from Thirsk in one morning. Do let me call Elizabeth to help you to your room while I prepare you some calming tea to help you fall asleep." While less adamant in her refusal this time, Mrs Turner tried again to protest; however, Mrs Watson would not give up. "No, no. Of course, you must be absolutely exhausted." And she continued to coax her sister-in-law even as she opened the door and called for Elizabeth.

Mrs Watson would have felt guilty for using Elizabeth in such a way if she did not know her eldest daughter so well. Elizabeth was a natural at taking care of people, and she was a great favourite with her aunt. While she enjoyed speaking, she was also a great listener and took pleasure in hearing whatever anyone would tell her. She also knew just what to say to please people.

From the moment Elizabeth entered, she understood her mother's look of fatigue from dealing with Mrs Turner, whom she knew her mother disliked, and said, "My dear aunt, please allow me to help you to your room, and, perhaps, you might be willing to tell me more of the fashions and parties of London, for you have the greatest taste and always give so many particulars that I almost feel like I am a part of it all."

It was done. Elizabeth's honest interest and flattery won her aunt's approval, and she was willingly led away to her room.

Mrs Watson breathed a sigh of relief and slumped over, wishing to sit down—or to simply lie down and refuse to leave her bed until their guests parted. However, she could do neither and, turning to her husband and brother-in-law, said, "Now, you boys play nice," before she turned towards the kitchen to prepare the promised tea.

Chapter Two

A Proposal

Mrs Watson

When Mrs Watson returned to the dining room where she had left the men, they were speaking about the more manly interests of politics, the roads, and other such matters that Mrs Turner considered too coarse to mention; however, the tension in the room was still palpable. She sighed and made her way in with the extra tray of tea and sweets she had prepared to calm everyone's frayed nerves.

Once she had served the gentlemen and sat down, she took a long sip from her cup—ignoring the slight burning sensation in order to regain her composure. Then she set down the cup and began, "Now, brother, I would kindly appreciate if you would elaborate on what your wife so callously suggested earlier. For I cannot imagine that you came here believing we would happily hand over one of our beloved children without warning or reason."

Her tone was measured, yet it left no doubt in the minds of either gentleman that her continued hospitality was conditional upon his response.

Mr Turner gulped. Then he lifted his cup and drank down the whole contents in order to prepare himself. However, he drank too quickly and choked, sputtering and coughing into his handkerchief. The absurdity of his discomfort shattered the last of the tension in the room, and—once he had regained his composure and been served a fresh cup—Mr Watson continued the conversation in a more amiable tone.

"We understand, my dear brother, what my sister is like, and we do not hold you accountable for her behaviour; however, *you* must understand that the offer was rather sudden."

"We only wonder," continued his wife, "why you did not write to us sooner and give us some warning—of *both* your coming out of your way from London to see us and of your interest in our children."

Mr Turner blushed deeply and apologised to them both. "My wife," he started before turning to Mr Watson, "your sister," he continued in a pleading tone, "told me that she had written to you—of both matters—before we left London. I had considered that it might be wise to add my own words to her letter, but she assured me that she posted it before I could write, and she kept us quite busy in those last few days. I…" he trailed off for a moment and sighed. "I only realised the truth of the matter once she had said her piece. Your expressions told me everything I should have already known, and I sincerely hope that you can forgive my negligence."

The couple shared a look, and Mrs Watson shook her head in exasperation. "While I know it is not your fault, you must know how she is after all these years. She is especially lacking when it comes to writing letters. I swear we do not receive half of the missives she claims to have sent."

Mr Turner nodded and sighed. "I do know, but you must understand that she is not so remiss in writing and replying to letters while we are in London among all the hustle and bustle of the season. I confess, her activity in that quarter when in town causes me to completely drop my guard with her."

Mr Watson smiled wryly at his brother-in-law while patting his wife's arm in a similar sort of reassuring manner to the one she had used earlier. "Then," he said to the former, "would you be kind enough to elaborate on this offer and what brought it about?"

Mr Turner nodded and explained as his wife had failed to.

"I admit that this whole debacle was my own doing," Mr Turner said before sighing again. "As you know, your sister and I have been married for well over a decade with no sign of children. As her brother, it may be uncomfortable for you to hear what I have to say, but, the truth is, that she has not often—that is to say—she does not…" he turned red again and stopped to take another large gulp of tea. Then he cleared his throat and said, "She has not been eager to share my bed."

The Watsons were shocked into silence, but it was Mrs Watson who first recovered and spoke. "Dear brother, I am not sure—that is to say, it may still be possible to beget a child if you truly want one."

They all sat in thought for a long moment. The shift in conversation had reignited the tension, but its cause was now entirely different.

Eventually, Mr Turner broke the silence with a weary chuckle. "No," he finally said. "No, I have long given up on such a thing. After my father passed away, my brother Gregory inherited the baronetcy at only eighteen. As you know from my letters, he took his time in looking for a wife and only married a few years back—nearly two decades after our father's death. Perhaps he hoped to leave the duty of providing heirs to me or our younger brother William; however, knowing how many children my parents lost before finally managing to raise three healthy sons, I was not surprised when none were forthcoming, though I felt a responsibility to try. But then, Gregory finally took matters into his own hands—he has sired an heir, who is now a hale and hearty boy of nearly four, and they are expecting another child in the autumn. Therefore, I no longer feel the need to coax my unwilling wife."

Mr Watson was uncertain what to say when the woman in question was his own sister, but he understood how difficult it must be for Mr Turner to speak about such matters in the first place, so he simply listened and encouraged his brother-by-marriage to continue.

"I have been considering the issue of my own heir for some time, and I mentioned it to my wife while we were in town. My father left my younger brother and myself just two thousand pounds apiece on his death. When I chose to use my small fortune to go into trade rather than entering university and the church as was planned for me, my mother and brothers cut all ties. It was only after many years, when I greatly increased my fortune through hard work and careful investments that my family found it in their hearts to speak to me again."

It was a terrible story, but Mr Turner told it with more sad humour than bitterness. Mr Watson and his wife were aware of much of his family background, but they had not realized how far Mr Turner had actually come on his own merit. His strength of character was no surprise to them, as it took someone with great self-control to live with a woman like Mrs Turner, but his story had still not answered all their questions.

It was Mrs Watson who voiced her thoughts, "I understand that you have been through a lot to get where you are today, and it is something to be admired. However, you have already spoken of your brother's expected increase in family, and I believe your sisters also have children who you could consider. So, why is Mrs Turner insisting on taking one of ours?"

"Can you not understand why, sister dear?" he said with a slow and sad smile that made Mrs Watson's heart ache for his plight both past and present.

"Even with the treatment I received from my family, I did not—and still do not—wish to break ties with them completely. However, my sisters married quite well, and their children are all provided for. My older brother inherited all the family estates and most of the family's fortune which will supply his children with everything they need. And William is still unmarried and, with his proclivities, is unlikely to do so; therefore, I need not worry about him." He paused then to consider his next words. "Honestly, if I may say so to a man of God whom I know reveres all his teachings—especially those regarding one's duties to family, the truth is that I have no wish to leave my fortune to any of them."

The Watsons were startled by the gravity of his tone—and the finality of his words. They had never imagined Mr Turner, whose patience and generosity were secretly envied by Mrs Watson, could sound so inflexible.

Their guest smiled at their expressions with a glint of the good-natured humour they knew him for. "It is not that I do not love my family, for they are just that—family. It is only that I have no wish of handing over what I have to those who would never truly be able to appreciate it as more than their due. They will care nothing for the hard work that it took to earn it."

He stopped to drink his tea, which his hostess had continued to fill without noticing it had gone cold due to her focus being entirely on Mr Turner and his story. He truly smiled for the first time now. "When I married your sister, I had thought myself a lucky man to find a woman who appreciated my hard work and resourcefulness, but I was soon made aware of how mistaken I was. However, all was not in vain."

He looked back up from his cup to his hosts. "While my wife may have only married me for my fortune and my potential to inherit a title, our marriage was not a complete disaster. I gained the acceptance of a true family in my bond to the both of you and in our other sister, Mrs Parker, and her husband. While I do not wish to deprive you of one of your children, I know that Parker has already chosen his heir from among his sister's sons, so I only thought it right to make you the offer. I may have given up on ever holding a child of my own blood, but it does not mean that I have given up on fatherhood altogether. I ask only that you be willing to consider trusting me with the care of one of yours."

Chapter Three

Considerations

Mr Watson

Mr Turner's story had been a lot to take in, and it was soon after decided that they would leave the matter to rest for the time being. The Turners had planned to remain for up to a fortnight if the Watsons did not mind hosting them, and—with so much to consider—the latter agreed.

While Mrs Watson was, at first, adamantly against the idea of sending one of their children to live with the Turners, her husband soon convinced her of the value of at least considering it.

"I am not pleased with the idea any more than you are, my love; however, it is not a bad proposal."

Cassandra had been sitting at her mirror and combing out her tresses to prepare for bed when he spoke. She turned on him like an angry Fury, "You cannot be serious, Robert. It was hard enough to watch each of them go off to school for so long without being able to do more than write. It is the worst with Robbie who has become so distant from us after spending so much of every year away from home. Now you wish me to give up one of my children for good? And to your youngest sister of all people?"

While he found his wife's anger terrifying, it was also a sight to behold. Though she was only two years shy from reaching her fifth decade, he could not help but think how beautiful she was—especially when she was cross. It was as if she lit up the space around her with the same passion and vibrancy that had attracted him to her in the first place, and he fell in love with her all over again. He walked over to her as she stood, too heated to remain seated, and he wrapped her in his embrace. She stiffened and stood frozen for a minute or two before she finally breathed a sigh and relaxed into his warmth.

Mrs Watson lifted her arms to return her husband's gentle hug and began to weep into his shoulder. "I cannot, Robert. I cannot imagine a life without all our little blessings here with us."

He ran a comforting hand over her hair and back as he tried to soothe away her fears and pain. "I understand, my love. Yet we must remember that one day soon, they will leave our home behind to create one for themselves."

Mrs Watson harrumphed into his chest, and he chuckled at her childish rebuttal.

"I do not want to think on it. They are all my little babies, and they always will be." Her tone was petulant, but it also held the humour that he understood to mean she realised how nonsensical she was being.

"They will always be *our* little blessings, my love. However, do you not hope for the day that they will bring their own little darlings into the world and make you a grandmother?"

She froze again, but then she slowly pulled away from him and gave him a serious look. "I am far too young yet to be anyone's grandmother," she said with mock annoyance, and then the both of them were laughing so hard they had to use the other for support.

He tucked her under the chin and grinned. "That is better. While I love your fiery nature, a smile always suits you best."

Her smile turned wry at his remark, and she embraced him once more and sighed. "I understand that Edward's fortune is a good one, and that, despite your sister's spending, he manages his income quite well, so any child they take in will have both wealth and a good, albeit small, estate one day. But," she looked up and met his eyes, "does it really need to be one of ours?"

Mr Watson looked longingly into his wife's eyes. He had done his best to save over the years, and their mutual families had been loyal patrons to them and their children—providing them more opportunities than he ever could have on his own. However, with their large family and the living's available means of improvement having reached its zenith, he had found no means of increasing their fortune in several years. With a world-weary sigh, he closed his eyes and pressed his forehead gently to hers in a silent communion of shared sorrow and solace.

"I am sorry that I could not offer you more, my love," he murmured, his voice barely above a whisper.

She shook her head against his chest and squeezed him tight. He knew then that she understood the truth of the matter. The Turners had so much to offer, and whichever child they chose to take would also have the ability in the future to aid the others more than either of their parents could.

Mrs Watson

For the next fortnight, the Turners would stay and observe the children. Robert Jr, who was the close friend and confidant of his cousin Charles, had been invited to spend the first half of the summer holiday with the latter at *Perlintun*, and so he was not at home to be considered. Meanwhile, Elizabeth helped with managing the household, controlling her younger siblings and managing their squabbles, visiting parishioners, and caring for their young Turner cousins at *Kyrkelidun*. Mr Turner decided that, though they both enjoyed her company, she was indispensable to her parents, and Mrs Turner did not seem to mind his decision—though Mrs Watson was sure that she only capitulated because she was hoping for a child who was less settled in their education. Either way, the two eldest Watson children were almost immediately disqualified as potential heirs.

Penelope—who had just completed her first year at seminary, and Maggie, or Margaret—who was Mrs Turner's goddaughter and namesake, were considered by Mrs Watson as the most likely candidates. Her guess seemed to be correct when Mrs Turner spoke to her about them one afternoon as they strolled through the gardens on the grounds of the main house.

"Your middle daughters possess most agreeable manners in company, and display a delightful desire to please me. I confess my particular regard for little Margaret, who, as my own goddaughter, does hold a singular place in my heart—as you must be aware. Indeed, I have frequently expressed to my dear Mr Turner how fortunate she is to be blessed with such a godmother as myself—whom, one might venture to suggest, is a godmother of unparalleled excellence and virtue."

Mrs Watson wanted to scoff, but she only allowed herself to force a smile and a nod before she turned away with the excuse of observing some flowers. For Mrs Turner seemed to have little interest in any child, let alone her own goddaughter. She had only thought of her little namesake a handful of times in the last nine years, and Mrs Watson wondered if the woman would remember her daughter's name if they did not share the same one. For her sister-in-law could barely remember the name of her eldest nephew, even though he shared a Christian name with her own brother. She had also referred to Elizabeth as 'Isabella', Penelope as 'Letitia', Sam as 'the boy child', and little Emma was only ever called 'the little mousy one' or 'the dear child' depending on her whims. Mrs Watson turned her face to roll her eyes at the ridiculous woman before she reminded herself that Mrs Turner would most likely be the benefactor of one of her children. So, she took in a deep breath and turned back to hear the end of the woman's soliloquy on her own self-proclaimed brilliance.

When she stopped to breathe, Mrs Watson cut in with, "I have noticed how fond Margaret is of you, and she has taken a great interest in all you have said of your estate and your travels." While she did not like the idea of what sort of influence Mrs Turner might have over little Maggie—whom she worried was already too similar in character to the older woman, she knew that Penelope—whose odd way of speaking and habit of staring too intensely at people—unnerved her aunt Turner and was unlikely to be her choice. However, the thought did amuse her from time to time, and Mrs Turner did have a strange fascination with speaking to the girl despite her clear distaste for Penelope's odd mannerisms.

Mrs Turner seemed very pleased with Mrs Watson's observation. "It should occasion no surprise, to be sure, that Margaret's regard should incline towards the fair prospect of our estate. For Shropshire possesses advantages far exceeding those of Yorkshire in every particular, and—as for travel—she can scarce hope to venture beyond such provincial towns as Redcar and Middleborough should she remain here. Alas, with a father quite unable to provide his daughters with even the smallest of dowries, the prospect of dinners, balls, and—someday—a proper season will always remain no more than a distant dream."

Mrs Watson bit her tongue to hold back her response. Mrs Turner always took every opportunity she could get to boast about the differences in their fortunes. She especially enjoyed needling at her brother's pride, and Mrs Watson was not sure she could manage many more days in the woman's company. She decided her best option for remaining civil was to return to her usual habit when in company with the woman. After all, Mrs Turner loved to speak, and to speak of herself at that. Mrs Watson need only show the barest semblance of listening while doing her best to block out the noise with more useful thoughts.

Chapter Four

The Chosen One

Mrs Watson

August 1787

It was only two days later when Mrs Turner, seemingly decided on her course, had presented Maggie with a pearl necklace after breakfast: "Merely a trifle I have been holding on to—though it possesses no particular value to me now, as I am already in possession of several such items," she had stated with a dismissive wave of her hand, as though she were a queen bestowing a paltry gift upon a vassal. Maggie, however, had clearly been thrilled and likely had hoped that she could someday be the owner of so many lovely jewels that she would not even care if one was lost or given away.

Maggie had spent the rest of the morning walking about bragging to all in sundry of her present, of her godmother's preference, and of her future good fortune. She had offered to let her sisters see the item, only to pull it away should they try to touch it and then tsk at their "dirty hands wanting to touch her pretty jewels."

This behaviour persisted through the day and well into the evening, showing no sign of abating even after dinner.

Mrs Watson knew her children well. She could see that Elizabeth was exasperated with her sister's antics while Penelope was ignoring her until later in the day, when she happened to comment, "If dirt is your concern, Maggie, you might want to check the hem of your dress." Meanwhile, Sam showed no interest in the matter, and Emma was becoming discouraged by her sister's refusal to even let her look at the 'pretty baubles'.

Before supper, Mrs Watson had already decided to confiscate the pearls after Maggie went up to bed when the same gift became the catalyst for disaster.

They were all sitting in the parlour with the grownups on one side conversing and the children playing together on the other side of the room.

Maggie was sitting quietly at one side, admiring her gift when she heard her siblings laughing together. It was only then that she noticed they had begun to play together without her. So, she made her way over to them and sat herself next to Emma.

"Well, Emma," she began, "do you like my pearls?"

Emma only stared at her sister without speaking.

Maggie huffed and tried again. "Do you want to touch them?"

Emma looked at her with distrust and continued to say nothing.

"Look here," Maggie continued, taking off her gift for the first time that day and holding the pearls out to her little sister. "You want to see them, right?"

Emma watched her sister carefully, and—with the necklace now only inches from her face—she lit up and reached for them. However, just as Emma's hands got close to the pearls, Maggie slapped them away.

"Don't touch it!" she exclaimed. "I said only that you could see it. Little girls with grubby hands cannot touch pretty things." Then she turned around and laughingly asked Penelope, "Do you want to see them?"

Mrs Watson was the first of the adults to notice the disturbance. She heard Maggie's shout and looked over in time to see little Emma quietly burst into tears. Then she stood to remonstrate with her next youngest daughter, but she was too late.

Penelope's gaze was fixed on Emma as Elizabeth reached over to pull their youngest sibling onto her lap and coo soothingly over her. Then Penelope stood and lunged at Maggie. A brawl between the two ensued, the likes of which Mr and Mrs Watson had become used to over the years, and she felt more than saw her husband rise from his chair and follow her over to the girls even as Mrs Turner's shrieks of "Oh my heavens!" and "What a commotion! I declare I have never—" rent the air, but Mrs Watson did not hear what came after, for her focus was solely on her children now.

Elizabeth pulled Emma and Sam out of the way to make room, and, as was the couple's way, Mrs Watson grabbed Penelope while her husband grappled with Maggie.

They had learned early on that, when their two middle daughters were provoked, Penelope would direct her anger at a certain target while Maggie would lash out at anyone and anything nearby. Therefore, for the safety of his wife, Mr Watson insisted that she should leave him to handle the younger girl. The separation of the sisters, however, was not a smooth one. Just as Mrs Watson was sure that they could keep things from escalating, Penelope managed to latch on to the pearl necklace and with the force of their parents pulling them apart—it snapped.

There was a moment of silence as everyone froze, and only the *tink*, *tink-tink*, *tinkity-tink* of the pearls falling and bouncing off the floor could be heard. Then the silence was broken as both Margarets rent the air with their screeching protestations.

Though Mr Watson had removed his charge from the room entirely, taking her to the bedroom she shared with her younger siblings to try to speak with her away from the others, it had taken a long time to calm her when her aunt's own howls had still been permeating the whole house.

Mrs Watson had seemed to have better luck as her charge had been completely calm after being led to the room she and Elizabeth shared. However, try as she might, Mrs Watson had not been able to get Penelope to admit to any fault in how she had handled the matter, nor had she convinced her to apologise to her younger sister.

In the end, they had not been able to do more than to send the two girls to bed with only bread and cheese for supper while they had returned to the parlour to clean up the mess and try to calm the still hysterical Mrs Turner.

"Good heavens, what a *dreadful* commotion!" their guest continued to exclaim even as they sat at table to sup. "I vow, never in my life have I been subjected to such an ill-natured spectacle. How can you permit such riotous conduct from your offspring, especially in the presence of company? To think that I had considered, albeit briefly, the possibility of welcoming such an unruly child into my *own* home. Such violence will never be countenanced under *my* roof," Mrs Turner ranted and raved about the girls' misconduct even long after supper was finished and the children had been sent up to bed.

Mr and Mrs Watson shared a look. Mr Watson had often told his wife about the squabbles between Mrs Parker and Mrs Turner when they were young—which, by his own reckoning, were on par with, or worse than, those between their two middle daughters. Unlike Penelope and Margaret who had three years between them and fought less the older they became, Mr Watson's youngest sisters were not even two years apart in age and did not grow out of their worst rows until long after they left the nursery.

After another quarter hour of complaints, Mrs Turner finally calmed down enough to move on.

"Alas," she said glibly as her voice changed back to normal, and she took on an almost predatory grin as she continued, "one cannot deny that some small advantage did, perhaps, arise from this unfortunate entanglement."

Her words left the other three in stunned silence which she almost seemed to expect as her grin grew into a self-satisfied smile. "My decision has been made."

"Your decision on what exactly?" asked Mr Watson as his wife felt a sinking pit of dread well up inside her at Mrs Turner's clear delight.

"On what, you ask?" She scoffed incredulously. Then she closed her eyes, placing her fingers to her temple, and gave another long-suffering sigh as if their confusion in her sudden change of topic was an inconceivable burden to her. "I must, of course, signify that I have come to a resolution regarding which of your offspring shall receive the honour of being brought up as the heiress to our considerable fortune."

"Heiress? Are you sure you still wish to take in Maggie after all you have said—"

Mrs Turner scoffed, interrupting her brother mid-sentence. "Such a one as she? 'Tis a notion I shall not even entertain. Nay, neither she, nor Lopie's namesake, shall be afforded any such opportunity, I vow. For, as I have previously stated, such impropriety shall find no allowance within my own home."

"Then what about young Samuel?" Pressed her husband with some hope that they may yet take home a boy child.

"La! Good heavens, no. What a preposterous notion! Have I not cautioned you regarding young gentlemen of tender years? They possess a spiritedness akin to untamed creatures—even more awful than what we have had the misfortune to observe this day, I daresay. How could you possibly conceive of my sharing our home with such a one? Pray, were you not at my very side, a mere three days ago, when he returned home with a toad secreted within his pocket? It was a most hideous creature, I must confess! And he wished to keep it within the very house as a pet, of all things. Nay, I fear I could never countenance the raising of a boy."

"Then—you cannot mean…" Mrs Watson was nearly white as a sheet as she realised the answer.

"The smallest one. The dear creature will be the lucky child."

"Emma," said Mr Watson in a regretful tone.

"Indeed. Emma shall inherit all that we possess—a most fortunate prospect, I daresay. Her virtues, no doubt, shall render her a most agreeable companion to us both."

"But why does it need to be Emma?" asked Mrs Watson pleadingly—hoping Mrs Turner would reconsider. "You have already seen that both Penelope and Margaret can behave well enough. It is only when they are together that issues like today's arise."

While Mrs Watson did not wish to lose any of her children, she hoped her sister-in-law would at least choose one who was old enough to understand the benefits of the prospect. She also knew that her middle daughters would benefit the most from being removed from each other's company. However, it had never crossed her mind that Mrs Turner would choose her youngest child, a girl only just five years old, a girl whose name she could not even remember. While Mrs Watson did not play favourites with her children, Emma was her last, her youngest and littlest blessing. She had not even considered the idea of being forced to part with her even for the purpose of her education for many years yet.

"During that unfortunate discord amongst your middle daughters, I could not help but observe Miss Emma. The dear child—silent save for the occasional sob—expressed her distress most tenderly. Even after you had removed those less tempered children, she continued to weep with admirable restraint. Indeed, such a well-behaved and quiet disposition is precisely what we have been seeking. Surrounded by so many offspring, madam, I confess I entertained hopes that one amongst them might suit our requirements, and it appears dearest Emma is that most fortunate child."

Mrs Watson would be loath to admit to what happened next, as all she wished to do was to grab her sister-in-law and shake her until she saw sense; however, what really happened was far different. for she fainted dead away in her own parlour.

Chapter Five

Farewells

Mr Watson

Three days after Mrs Turner announced her decision, the morning of Emma's departure dawned with a stillness that seemed to suffocate the household. Mrs Watson had barely slept and had risen before the sun, her movements slow and deliberate as she folded the last of Emma's few dresses into a small trunk. Mr Watson watched from the doorway; his throat tight. He had rehearsed the practical arguments—a better future, fine clothes, riding lessons, a fortune—but none of them eased the weight in his chest as his wife pressed a new, little ragdoll, a final parting gift to her daughter, to her chest, her shoulders shaking silently.

He walked over and took her into his arms for what seemed like the hundredth time since his sister had come and turned their lives upside down with her proposal. She turned into him and wept. It took all of his strength to hold back his own tears. They would only do more harm than good in the circumstances.

"My love," he tried to speak, but his voice faltered. He stood there, resigned to remain silent.

After several minutes, his wife's crying ceased, and her stifled sniffles were all that filled the quiet room. Finally, she spoke.

"I know," she squeezed him hard. "I know it is for her own good, but…" She paused and looked up at him with her grief still visible in the watery edges of her eyes. "I cannot help but think that it is not too late to change our minds. Turner may still wait for his brother to provide more children, they might change their minds and choose another once they are older, we might find some little ways to live more frugally—" her words were now spilling out in a jumble of thoughts, and he knew not what to say to her. He simply pulled her close once more and let her release all her worries.

They stood that way for some time before small noises from the stairs told them that they were no longer the only ones awake. Mrs Watson pulled away and fixed her rumbled gown before wiping her face.

"I'll go check on the preparations for breakfast with Cook," she said hastily, and she was off.

He could only watch her go as Elizabeth came up behind him and put a hand on his arm. He looked down at her to see the sheen of tears on her face. He was not sure how much she had heard, but he knew she was aware of her mother's plight. The two of them had taken turns to encourage and console Mrs Watson over the last few days, but he worried it was not enough.

"I will go to her," said the most capable and stalwart of their children.

He looked at her with both pride and resignation. "Thank you, Lizzy dear."

She smiled through her tears. "It has been many years since you called me that, Papa." Then she patted his arm and followed her mother into the kitchen.

He remained standing there alone for some time, lost in thought.

He still remembered clearly when, a little over a month after Robbie had gone off to school and only two days after Elizabeth's ninth birthday, she had come into the parlour one evening after helping put the others to bed.

She had stood tall and told them, *"Now that I am the oldest child at home, with four younger siblings to look after, I'm all grown up. From now on, I will no longer be Lizzy but Elizabeth. I already told the children, so I wanted to let you know."* Then she had leaned forward to kiss them both goodnight and informed her mother on her way out, *"You don't need to come tuck me in. I'm a big girl now."*

He also remembered how his wife's face had scrunched up as she tried to smile and stay strong only long enough to accept her daughter's decision and see her off before she had burst into tears. She had told him later, *"It is the first time I have realised how quickly our children are growing up. I had hoped it would be at least a few more years before I would need to consider such things."*

Accepting that their children were growing up and, one day, would no longer need them was a bitter pill to swallow.

Mrs Watson

The carriage waited in the drive, its polished wood and brass fittings gleaming in the morning light. Emma stood between her parents with her siblings lined up next to them, her small hand clutching the new ragdoll to her chest. She was not crying, but her eyes were wide and bewildered as she watched her things being taken out of the house and lifted into the carriage.

Mr Watson patted her on the head and said, "You must listen to your aunt and uncle Turner, Emma dear. They will write to us with any message you wish to send until you are able to write us letters on your own, and we shall see you as soon as we are able to."

Emma nodded mutely, her confused expression showing her parents that she didn't quite understand. *How could she?* thought Mrs Watson, her tears barely contained as she watched the scene. *At five, the world is a place of certainties—her mother's lap, her sister's stories, the creak of the stairs outside her room. Now, she is being sent away, and no amount of gentle words can make it right. My darling—my dear, sweet, poor little Emma.*

While she may not understand, Emma seemed keenly aware of the tension as she clung to her mother's skirt. Mrs Watson leaned down and put her hand on her daughter's cheek. Her voice was steady, if strained as she said, "You are to live with your aunt and uncle Turner now, my dear. They will care for you as we do, and you shall want for nothing."

Emma's lower lip began to tremble as she replied to her mother's words with, "But why only me, Mama?" The question hung between them, unanswerable. Mrs Watson looked into Emma's eyes with her own red-rimmed ones and smoothed her daughter's hair.

"Because they chose you, my dear," was all her mother could manage before she stepped back. The words sounded hollow even to her, but Emma only nodded unwillingly, her small fingers now twisting the hem of her pinafore.

Elizabeth stepped forward then, her own eyes bright with unshed tears. "You must be very brave, Emma, and make sure, like Papa said, that you mind Aunt and Uncle Turner. They will treat you very well." She hugged her sister and added, "Remember that we all love you so very much," as she stepped back. Emma only stared at her, her face starting to show a hint of worry as her grip tightened on the doll.

Penelope, ever practical, approached Emma next. She reached into her pocket and pulled out a small, smooth stone—one she had found in the garden weeks ago and kept for no reason other than that it had pleased her. "Here," she said, pressing the stone into Emma's palm. "Here is something pretty that no one will take from you. Keep it so you will remember me." Emma looked down at the stone, then up at Penelope, before Penelope wrapped her up in a gentle hug.

As Margaret's turn to say goodbye came, she refused to budge. She remained a little apart from her older sisters with her arms crossed and huffed. "It's *not* fair. It should be *me. I'm* Aunt Turner's goddaughter. *I* was the one who was supposed to go with them!" she exclaimed and stomped her foot. Then she stomped up to stand before Emma who was now trembling and both of them began to tear up for different reasons. "*I* was the one who was supposed to get all the pretty dresses and jewels," she yelled, her face only inches from her younger sister's, "Why should it be *you* who gets them?"

Seeing the turn things were taking, Elizabeth bolted forward and grabbed Margaret before her mother could. Mrs Watson debated going after them as Elizabeth led her sister back inside, the latter complaining all the way; however, she could not leave without seeing her youngest off.

Mrs Watson turned back just in time to see Samuel, his face scrunched in confusion, tug at his father's coat. "Why is Emma leaving with Aunt and Uncle Turner, Father? Are we not going too?" he asked, his voice small. Mr Watson leaned over and explained to Samuel that Emma would be the only one going and they would not see her for some time. Sam's face became confused and sad. He looked at his sister, then darted forward and threw his arms around her. "I'll miss you, Emma. I don't want you to go. But I hope you won't forget me before we meet again," he mumbled into her hair. It was only now that Emma's face scrunched up, and she finally released the tears that had been accumulating in her eyes.

Mr Watson took his youngest son by the shoulders, leading him away from Emma to allow his wife a chance to step forward again and restore order to their farewells. But just as Mrs Watson knelt in front of her youngest daughter, Mrs Turner came out of the house.

Seeing that the carriage was ready to go, Mrs Turner cleared her throat. "Pray, child, make haste, for time shall not stop on your account. My dearest brother," she said turning back to look at him, "it has been a delight to visit you and yours once more, and I know not when fortune shall grant us another such opportunity." She turned again, "And you, my sweet sister, do not let your heart be troubled, for we possess the means to care for the child and to furnish her with advantages far exceeding anything she might aspire to in such a lamentable establishment as this." Then, with a pompous air, she turned and—with a swish of her skirts—made her way to the carriage, where the footman helped her in.

Mr Turner, who had followed his wife out, watched her performance with a bemused expression and shook his head. Then he turned back to his brother and sister-in-law and apologised once more for her behaviour. "Please take your time with your goodbyes. I will try to hold her off as long as possible," he said before following her into the carriage.

Mrs Watson leaned down and looked at her daughter's silently weeping face. "Do not worry, my love. You will go with the Turners, and they will give you many nice things—new dresses and dolls, and everything a little girl could wish for."

Emma, who was now crying in earnest, began to blubber, "W-w-why must I g-go? Why a-a-are you not all c-coming? I... I d-don't want to g-go. I w-want to stay h-h-here with ev-everyone." She somehow managed her laments between her sobs.

Mrs Watson could no longer hold back her own tears. Her breath hitched as she felt the warm liquid streaming down her cheeks, and she pulled her daughter into one last embrace. "Be good, my darling. Be good, and remember you will *always* be my littlest blessing."

Then she stood and turned quickly, allowing her husband to come and take her place. Mr Watson lifted Emma into his arms before conveying her to the carriage. Then he said his own final goodbye and gave her a kiss on the forehead before placing her inside. His hands lingered for just a moment longer on her waist before releasing her. Emma turned to look back at him as he stepped away from the carriage—closing the door and moving back to his wife's side.

Mrs Watson wrapped her arms around her husband's for support. Then she saw Emma's small face appear—pressed against the glass, her breath fogging the pane—before they heard the knock on the carriage. As the wheels began to turn, she kept her gaze fixed on that little face, memorising every line, as if she would never see her youngest child again.

And just like that, she was gone.

Once the carriage could no longer be seen, Mrs Watson's tears turned from silent weeping to piercing anguish. For a brief moment, Mr Watson only stood there stiffly. Then he embraced his wife and let his own tears spill and mix with hers. They continued in that manner for a long while.

Mrs Watson was unaware of the flow of time, but she eventually noticed that Elizabeth had returned to them, her own face streaked with the tears she had held back earlier. Soon after, Mrs Watson allowed her husband and eldest daughter to lead her back into the house and to her room, where the weight of her grief caused her to collapse into a fitful sleep.

Epilogue

Omniscient

After Emma left to live with the Turners in Shropshire, Mr Watson observed his wife's health falter under the sacrifice. The loss hit Mrs Watson even harder when she had to explain the circumstances of Emma's departure to their family, especially little Mary and Bethie Turner, the former who was the same age and the latter only a year younger than Emma. The two girls had been close playmates with the Watsons' youngest child, and their lack of understanding of the reasons for sending Emma off to live with the Turners only intensified the couple's guilt—sure that the pain and loss of the separation Emma's closest playmates felt could only mirror her own.

Meanwhile, their own children's reactions varied: Robert Jr received the news with indifference; Penelope seemed unaffected and soon after returned to school; Margaret railed against the injustice, loudly lamenting the loss of the fine dresses and jewels her godmother had promised, and often brought up her broken necklace whenever she felt cheated of anything; and Sam, now the youngest at home, mourned the loss of his playmate briefly but had reached an age where he preferred the company of the other boys of the parish. Elizabeth alone seemed to share her mother's grief, though she agreed the opportunity was for Emma's good.

Mrs Watson frequently lamented her choice to let her youngest go, and she was sure that Emma must be feeling the weight of her abandonment with each passing day. The strain of her sorrow soon manifested physically—she fell ill within days of Emma's departure, and it took several more for her to be able to climb out of bed and return to her daily chores. It took many weeks before she stopped calling for Emma when she reigned in the children from playing outdoors or to join them for meals. It was months before she could fall asleep without weeping over her nightly prayers for Emma's health and safety.

The letters began arriving as soon as the Turners reached the Peak District. Mr Turner wrote of Emma's shifting temperaments—from sullen silence to wide-eyed excitement at the views. While, after they arrived home, Mrs Turner wrote and confided in her letter that, "Emma has at last stopped sulking, which is something to be thankful for. I was afraid that I may have made the wrong choice—though at least she remained silent and otherwise well-behaved."

Over time, Mr and Mrs Watson appreciated that Mr Turner was by far the better correspondent between the two spouses. His letters described all the advantages they had given Emma that her parents could never afford for her or her siblings without the judgement and insults Mrs Turner's letters carried. Aside from the hiring of a governess, one Mrs Simms who came highly recommended, Emma was blessed with her own personal maid to serve her. There were also the constant gifts of gowns, shoes, hats, and other such accessories as well as new dolls and books.

Mr Watson missed his daughter deeply, yet he managed his grief with quiet resolve, comporting himself as ever. But Mrs Watson did not recover so easily. Watching her pale beneath the weight of her responsibilities, he wondered how he might ever repay the cost of her sacrifice.

After a half-year's absence, Mr Watson realised that the removal of only one child did little to increase their income, and he often found himself regretting their decision to send Emma to Shropshire.

Mr Watson finally gathered the courage to ask his wife if she wished to bring Emma back home. Yet the Turners' most recent letter—detailing their season in Bath and Emma's meetings with her aunt Parker and godmother, Miss Mordaunt—sealed their decision. Their youngest was better off where she was, no matter how fiercely they missed her, and Mrs Watson assured him there was nothing they could do for little Emma should she return to them. They could only pray for her continued good luck.

Though Emma was gone, her absence lingered. The house, once filled with the laughter of six children, now echoed with the silence of sacrifice—a silence that would soon be answered by an unexpected turn of fortune.

Before You Go

Did You Enjoy This Prequel?

If you enjoyed *The Watsons: Beginnings: Arc Two: Family & Fortune*, don't miss the rest of the series:

The Watsons: Beginnings: Arc One: Courtship & Marriage

The eBook is live on Amazon, Draft2Digital, and associated retailers

The Watsons: Beginnings: Arc Three: Living & Loss

(TBA)

Continue reading about the adventures of the Watson family in *Refined and Returned: A Completed Version of The Watsons by Jane Austen* in three Volumes by Eireanne Michaels.

Volume I

The eBook is live on Amazon only

The print book is live on Amazon, Draft2Digital, and associated retailers

You can also subscribe to my newsletter to be kept up to date on new releases and book or chapter previews at **Jane Austen's Literary Lasagna**.

https://jaliterarylasagna.wixsite.com/jane-austen-fandom

Preview

Arc 3: Prospects & Changes

England, 1789

Two years after Emma Watson left her family behind, the consequences of that single decision still linger in every corner of their home—but now another change stands before them.

Mrs. Watson continues to mourn the loss of her youngest daughter and the painful necessity that seemed to demand such a choice. Mr. Watson, in turn, carries a quiet guilt, having come to realize that the modest relief of one less mouth to feed was not worth the toll it has taken on his wife's health. Yet with letters arriving that speak of Emma's happiness and comfort in her new situation, the family resolves that it is time to look forward rather than back.

At this moment of transition, a letter arrives from Mr. Watson's long-time friend, Mr. Thomas Edwards of Dorking in

Surrey. The living of Stanton, soon to be vacant, may be secured, and it promises both respectability and the possibility of future improvement. Mr. and Mrs. Watson weigh their options carefully. In Yorkshire, they have the comfort of close relations and longstanding responsibilities, particularly toward the Turner children. Yet the prospect of increased income and a fresh beginning proves difficult to ignore. With the support of relatives and friends, and through the influence of Mr. Watson's brother-in-law, Lord Middleton, the offer of the living is secured without Mr. Watson's needing to travel south to present himself. Even so, many preparations remain before such a change can be accomplished.

This story follows the family's farewell to their long-time home and the familiar network of relations and friends who have shaped their daily lives, and traces the early stages of their journey south. Anyone who has endured days of travel with young children crowded into small carriages will readily imagine that the road is not an easy one. Delays, discomfort, and uncertainty attend them long before they reach their destination.

This prequel short offers readers a closer understanding of each member of the Watson family, revealing their individual temperaments and the bonds that unite them. As they leave behind a place where they are known and supported to settle in a town where they know almost no one, doubts begin to surface alongside hope. The physical journey from one county to another mirrors the deeper emotional passage from an established life into an unknown future.

Arc 3 explores this transition in full: the strain and promise of departure, the testing of family ties, and the uncertain first steps into a new chapter of their lives.

Author Bio

Eireanne Michaels is an introvert who is currently living in Korea among some of her rescue cats. She is one of those women who is perfectly happy to be considered a 'crazy cat lady' as it both keeps people away and is simply the unavoidable truth.

She is a fan of fantasy, science fiction, and old British literature. She has been a fan of Jane Austen's novels for many, many years (possibly 'since tigers were smoking' which is the Korean way to say 'since dinosaurs roamed the earth.')

To Eireanne, Austen's works are like good lasagna; it's full of layers that bring new delicious titbits to the surface each time they are reached. However, most people only notice the toppings and miss the real meat underneath. Jane Austen was not just a great author, she had depths that we may never fully discover. It has created a passion, or possibly obsession, in this author to uncover all of the hidden gems in her sarcastic and witty novels by slowly dissecting them and, occasionally, reimagining them.

So, for her own amusement, she has decided to take up writing JAFF in order to help her better understand the time period, the characters, and the original author. While she writes for herself, she knows that there are others who are interested in the many facets of Austen's works who might also enjoy her works, so she decided to share them.

Thank you for reading!

www.ingramcontent.com/pod-product-compliance
Lightning Source LLC
LaVergne TN
LVHW050943080826
845145LV00004B/1382
9781969841064